Dear Parent:

Congratulations! Your child is taking
the first steps on an exciting journey.
The destination? Independent reading!

STEP INTO READING® will help your child get there. The program offers
five steps to reading success. Each step includes fun stories and colorful art.
There are also Step into Reading Sticker Books, Step into Reading Math
Readers, Step into Reading Write-In Readers, Step into Reading Phonics
Readers, and Step into Reading Phonics First Steps! Boxed Sets—a complete
literacy program with something for every child.

Learning to Read, Step by Step!

Ready to Read Preschool–Kindergarten
• big type and easy words • rhyme and rhythm • picture clues
For children who know the alphabet and are eager to
begin reading.

Reading with Help Preschool–Grade 1
• basic vocabulary • short sentences • simple stories
For children who recognize familiar words and sound out
new words with help.

Reading on Your Own Grades 1–3
• engaging characters • easy-to-follow plots • popular topics
For children who are ready to read on their own.

Reading Paragraphs Grades 2–3
• challenging vocabulary • short paragraphs • exciting stories
For newly independent readers who read simple sentences
with confidence.

Ready for Chapters Grades 2–4
• chapters • longer paragraphs • full-color art
For children who want to take the plunge into chapter books
but still like colorful pictures.

STEP INTO READING® is designed to give every child a successful
reading experience. The grade levels are only guides. Children can progress
through the steps at their own speed, developing confidence in their
reading, no matter what their grade.

Remember, a lifetime love of reading starts with a single step!

For Mallory, my good buddy
—H.K.

www.stepintoreading.com

Educators and librarians, for a variety of teaching tools, visit us at
www.randomhouse.com/teachers

Library of Congress Cataloging-in-Publication Data
Kilgras, Heidi.
Me too, Woody! / by Heidi Kilgras ; illustrated by Philippe Harchy.
    p.   cm. — (Step into reading. A step 1 book)   "Toy Story 2."
SUMMARY: Jessie feels left out when Woody and Buzz play checkers and seesaw together,
but when they start a baseball game, she and the other toys get to join the game.
ISBN 0-7364-1266-2 (trade) — ISBN 0-7364-8004-8 (lib. bdg.)
[1. Toys—Fiction.]
I. Harchy, Philippe, ill.   II. Title.   III. Series: Step into reading. Step 1 book.
PZ7.K5553 Me 2003 [E]—dc21 2002013343

Printed in the United States of America 20 19 18 17 16 15 14 13 12

STEP INTO READING, RANDOM HOUSE, and the Random House colophon are registered
trademarks of Random House, Inc.

Disney · PIXAR

TOY STORY 2

Me Too, Woody!

by Heidi Kilgras

illustrated by Atelier Philippe Harchy

Random House 🏠 New York

Buzz and Woody.

Good buddies!

Game time.

Checkers!

"Me too, Woody!"

"No, only two."

Buzz and Woody.

Good buddies!

Playtime.

Seesaw!

"Me too, Woody!"

"No, only two."

Poor Jessie!

"Hey, Jessie."

"Want to play?"

"Yay!"

Play ball!

Big swing.

Big hit!

"Run, Buzz!"

"Run, Jessie!"

Going.
Going.

Got it!

Good play!
Good buddies!